TOO
NOISY!

*Listen while I tell you
all about a bunch of Bungles—
they're a great enormous family,
and they're noisy,
just too noisy!*

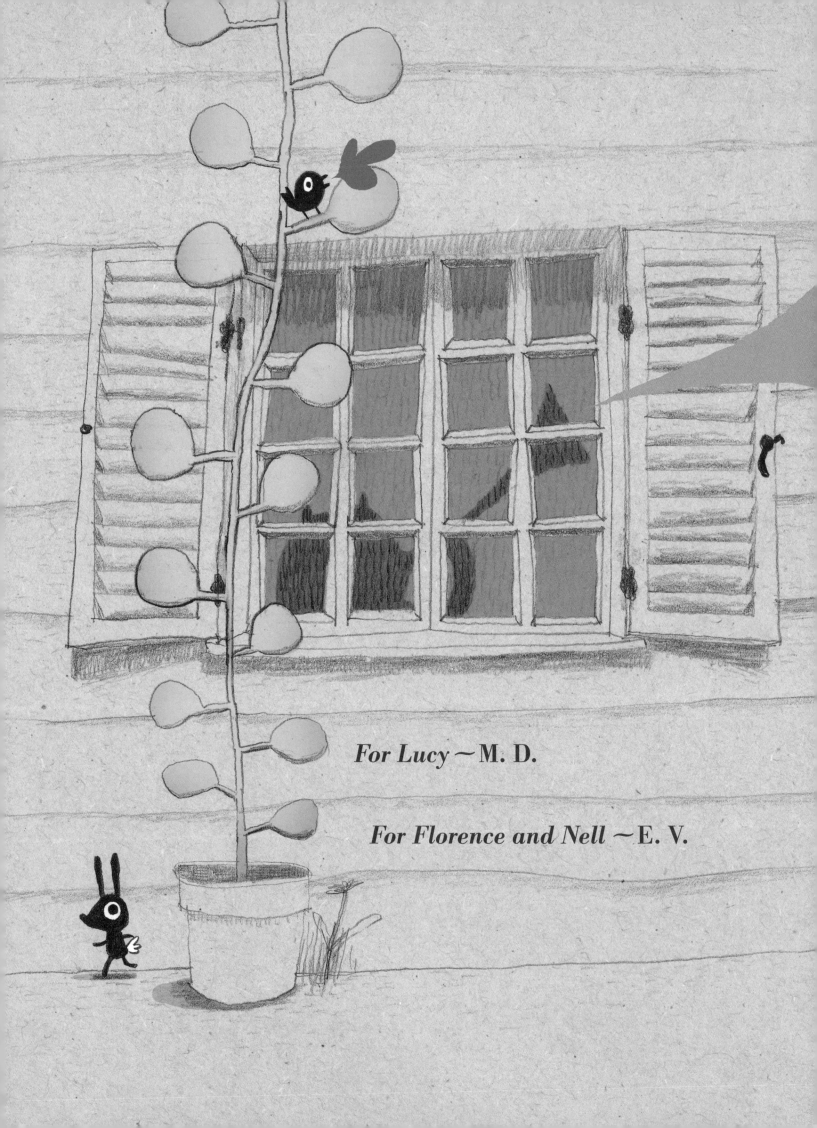

For Lucy ~ M. D.

For Florence and Nell ~ E. V.

TOO NOISY!

malachy doyle
ed vere

CANDLEWICK PRESS

CRASH! JANGLE!
Meet the Bungles—
Whistle! Tweetle! Toot!
Mama Bungle *trills* and *tinkles,*
Papa **wheezes,** then he **sneezes,**
Granny Bungle *clicks* and *clacks,*
and Grandpa Bill's a **boomer.**
Bella **bangs** on pots and pans,
and Fitz and Finn,
the Bunglebabies,
Squeak and
Squawk and
SQUELCH!

"Oh, will you ever shush!" cried Sam,
the middle one, the quiet one,
the Bungle full of dreams.
"Nobody can think around here,
all boom and bash and wallop!
I want it to be peaceful,
but it's not—it never is!"

And so he upped

and so he offed

to the woods.

and so he wandered

"Ahh!" he sighed.
"That's better," as he
looked around at clouds
and trees and greens
and blues and water.

He sat and looked,
and thought and looked,
and sat and hummed
a hum.

"*The sky is blue.
My shoe is, too!*"

"It rhymes!" said Sam.
"I like it!"

He had another little walk . . .
then sat and looked,
and thought and looked,
and sat and hummed again.

"I can see a funny tree—
It's all striped, like Mama B.!"

"It rhymes!" said Sam.
"I love it!"

Then Sam upped

and offed

and wandered

deeper, deep into the woods.

But **_"Eeek!"_**
He felt a
creepy-crawly
climbing up
his leg.

"Oooh," he said.
"It's dark," he said.
"I think I might be
lost," he said.

Then **"Beek!"**
He felt a flitter-flutter
flap around his face!
"Oooh," he said.
"I'm scared," he said.
"I wished I hadn't dared,"
he said, "to go off alone,
all on my own."

Then

"*Eeeky-beek!*"

A slippy-slidy

slithered

down his neck!

He opened up his lips,

and then he opened up his mouth,

and then he opened

up his throat

and *bellowed,*

"Help!
Help!
Help!

He listened
and he listened
and . . .

well, first
Sam heard a *little* sound—
a *trilling* and a *tinkling* . . .

then he heard a bigger sound—
a **wheezing** and a **sneezing** . . .
a **clicking** and a **clacking**,
then a **boomty-boomty-booming,**
growing **loud and loud again**

till it was like a . . .

HURRICANE
of NOISE!

The sun came through the trees,
and so did Mama Bungle, Papa Bungle,
Grandpa Bill and Granny, too,
Bella banging pots and pans
and Fitz and Finn, the Bunglebabies—
Squeak, **Squawk,** **SQUELCH!**

"It's Sam," they yelled.
"We've found him!"

And they gathered all around him,
and they hugged him and they kissed him,
and they said how much they'd missed him.
He said he'd missed them, too.
He said . . .

"Although you're very loud,
you crowd, I'm glad to be a Bungle!"

Well, everybody cheered,
"HOORAY!"

And Sam was oh so happy,
for he loved them, every one.

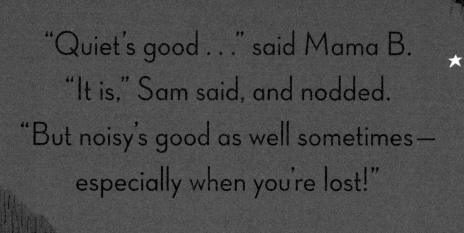

"Quiet's good . . ." said Mama B.
"It is," Sam said, and nodded.
"But noisy's good as well sometimes—
especially when you're lost!"

*And that's the ending,
happy ending.*

That's the end.